THIRTEEN

REMY CHARLIP & JERRY JOYNER

THE NEW YORK REVIEW CHILDREN'S COLLECTION, NEW YORK

THIS IS A NEW YORK REVIEW BOOK
PUBLISHED BY THE NEW YORK REVIEW OF BOOKS
435 HUDSON STREET, NEW YORK, NY 10014
WWW.NYRB.COM

LIBRARY OF CONGRESS CATALOGING-IN-PUBLICATION DATA
NAMES: CHARLIP, REMY, AUTHOR, ILLUSTRATOR. | JOYNER, JERRY, AUTHOR, ILLUSTRATOR.
TITLE: THIRTEEN / BY REMY CHARLIP AND JERRY JOYNER.
DESCRIPTION: NEW YORK : NEW YORK REVIEW BOOKS, [2018] | SERIES: NEW YORK REVIEW
    CHILDREN'S COLLECTION | ORIGINALLY PUBLISHED BY PARENTS' MAGAZINE PRESS IN 1975.
    | SUMMARY: THIRTEEN PICTURE STORIES OF A MAGIC SHOW, A SEA DISASTER, AND OTHER
    DRAMAS DEVELOP SEPARATELY BUT SIMULTANEOUSLY.
IDENTIFIERS: LCCN 2017045136| ISBN 9781681372303 (HARDBACK) | ISBN 9781681372310
    (EPUB)
SUBJECTS: LCSH: CHILDREN'S STORIES, AMERICAN. | CYAC: SHORT STORIES. | BISAC: JUVENILE
    FICTION / IMAGINATION & PLAY. | JUVENILE FICTION / CONCEPTS / SIZE & SHAPE. | JUVENILE
    FICTION / ART & ARCHITECTURE.
CLASSIFICATION: LCC PZ7.C3812 TH 2018 | DDC [E]—DC23
LC RECORD AVAILABLE AT HTTPS://LCCN.LOC.GOV/2017045136

ISBN 978-1-68137-230-3
AVAILABLE AS AN ELECTRONIC BOOK, ISBN 978-1-68137-231-0

MANUFACTURED IN CHINA. PRINTED ON ACID-FREE PAPER.

10 9 8 7 6 5 4 3 2 1

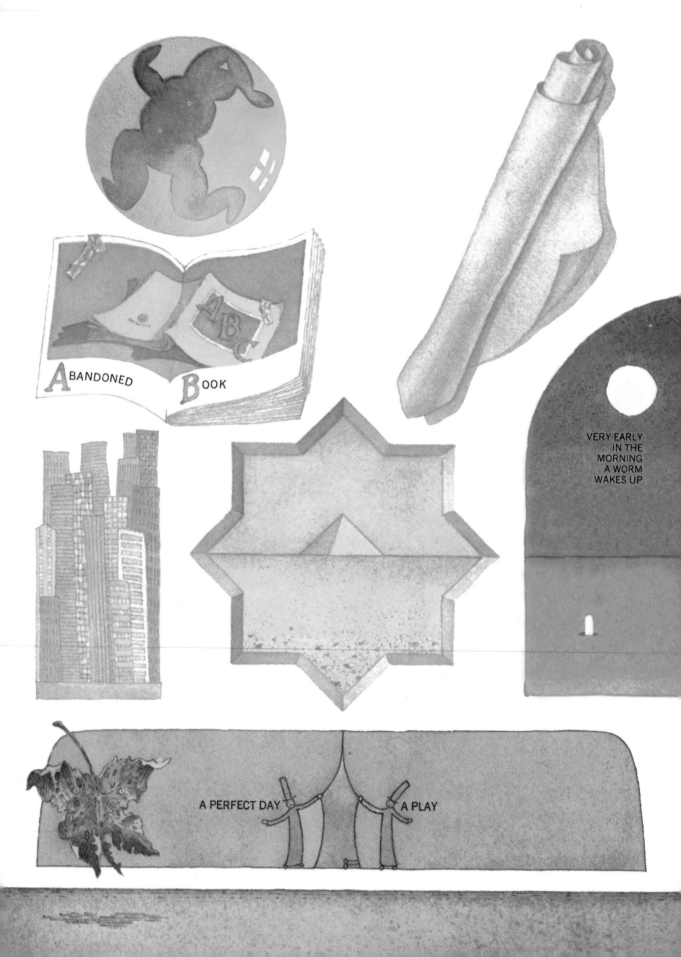

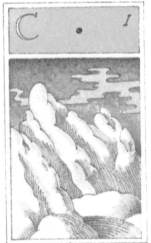

13

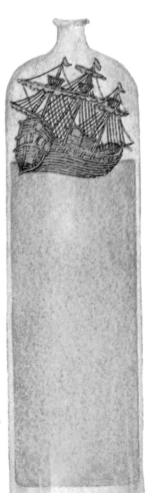

SWANS BECOMING WATER

VERY EARLY IN THE MORNING A WORM WAKES UP

THIS IS A VERY OLD SHIP.

IT DOESN'T FIT

12

11

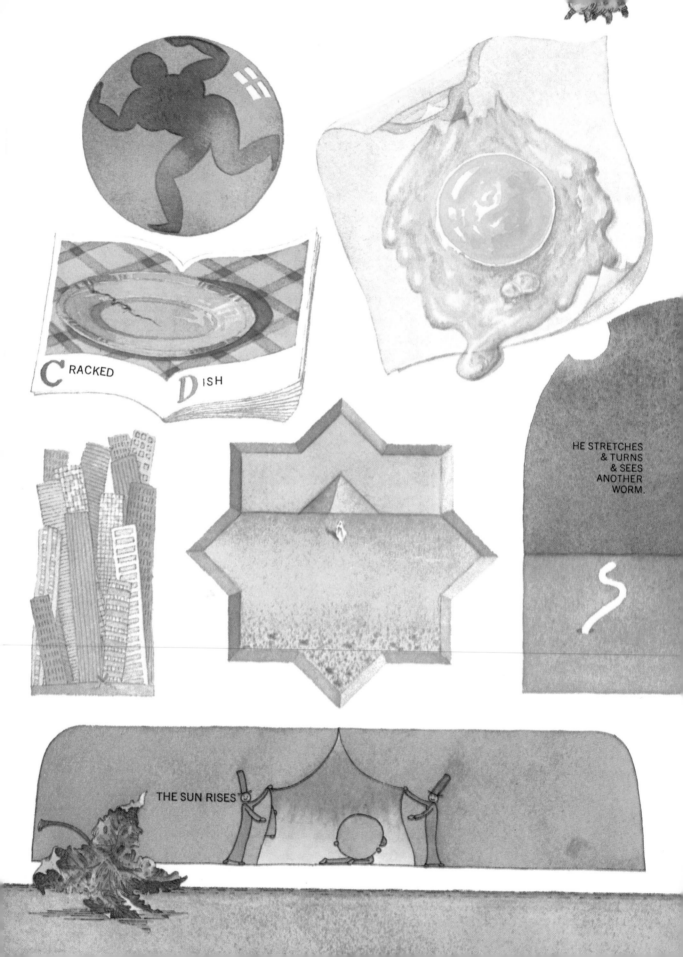

CRACKED **D**ISH

HE STRETCHES
& TURNS
& SEES
ANOTHER
WORM.

THE SUN RISES

12

WATER BECOMING STARS

IN FACT IT'S SO OLD IT CAN HARDLY FLOAT ANYMORE.

HE STRETCHES & TURNS & SEES ANOTHER WORM.

IT DOESN'T FIT

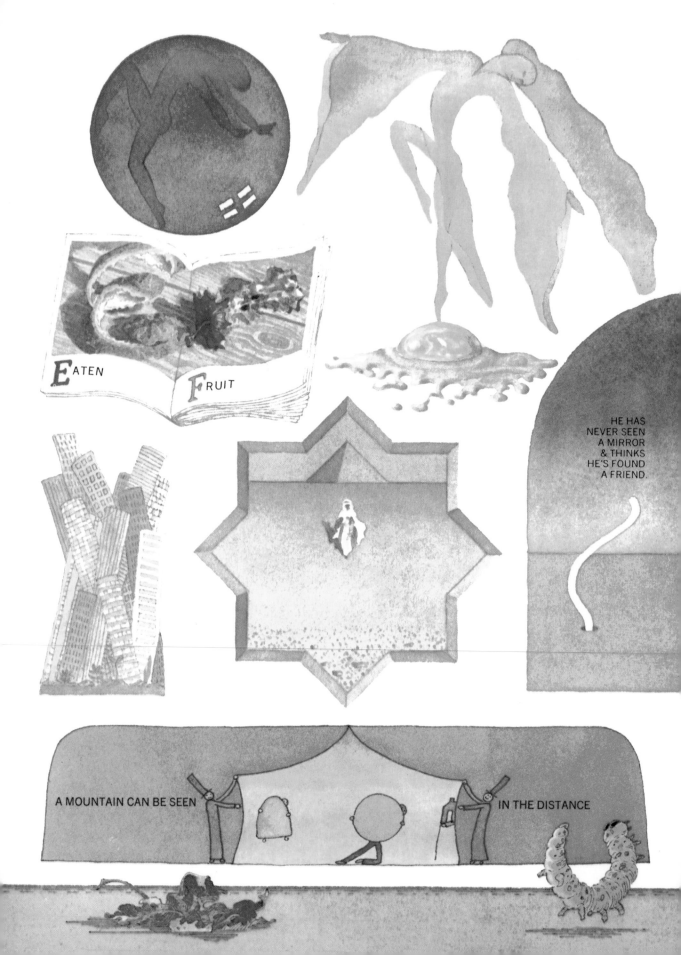

11

HE HAS NEVER SEEN A MIRROR & THINKS HE'S FOUND A FRIEND.

STARS BECOMING TREE

IN FACT IT'S SINKING.

IT DOESN'T FIT

10

9

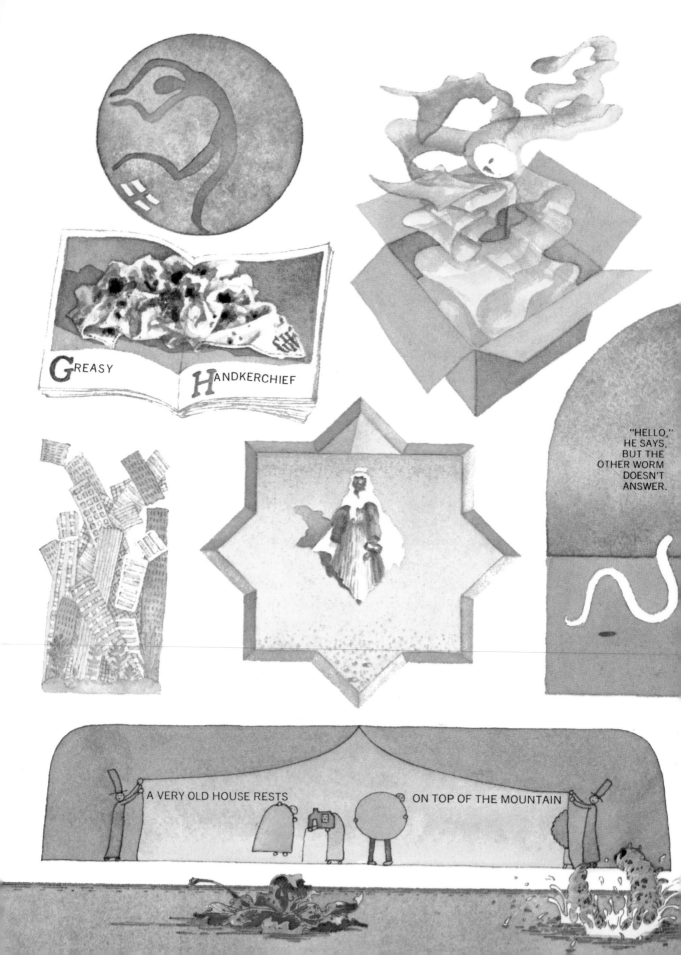

GREASY HANDKERCHIEF

"HELLO," HE SAYS, BUT THE OTHER WORM DOESN'T ANSWER.

A VERY OLD HOUSE RESTS ON TOP OF THE MOUNTAIN

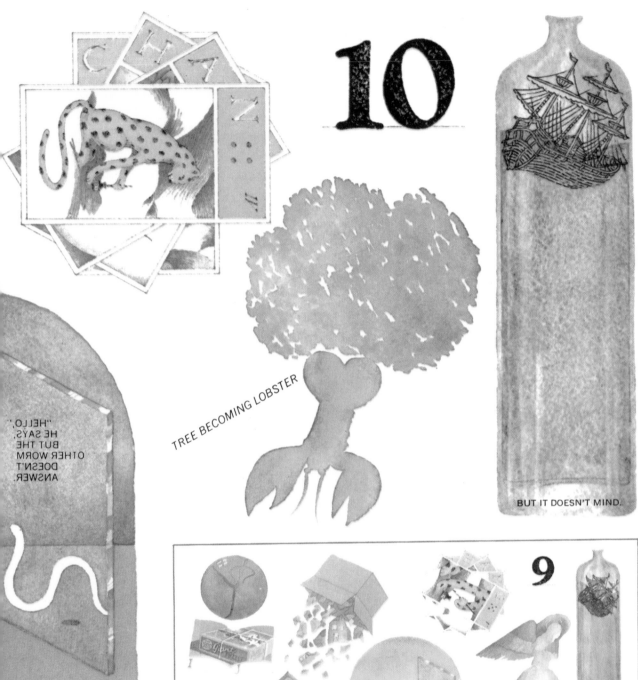

10

TREE BECOMING LOBSTER

BUT IT DOESN'T MIND.

"HELLO,"
HE SAYS,
BUT THE
OTHER WORM
DOESN'T
ANSWER.

IT DOESN'T FIT

9

8

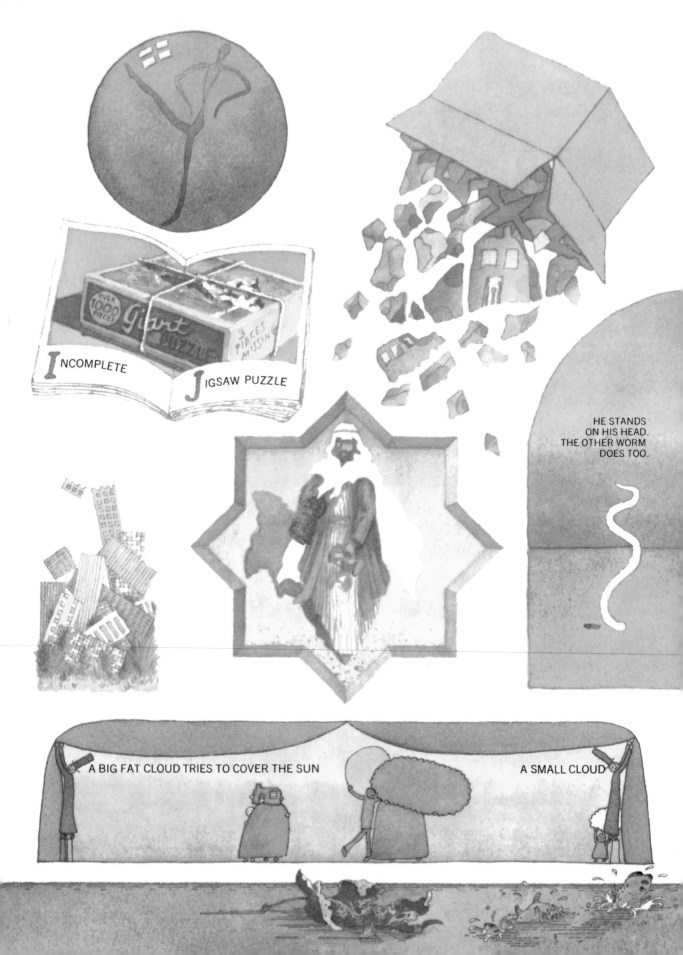

INCOMPLETE JIGSAW PUZZLE

HE STANDS
ON HIS HEAD.
THE OTHER WORM
DOES TOO.

A BIG FAT CLOUD TRIES TO COVER THE SUN

A SMALL CLOUD

9

LOBSTER BECOMING ANGEL

HE STANDS
ON HIS HEAD.
THE OTHER WORM
DOES TOO.

IT'S BEEN EVERYWHERE.

8

7

IT DOESN'T FIT

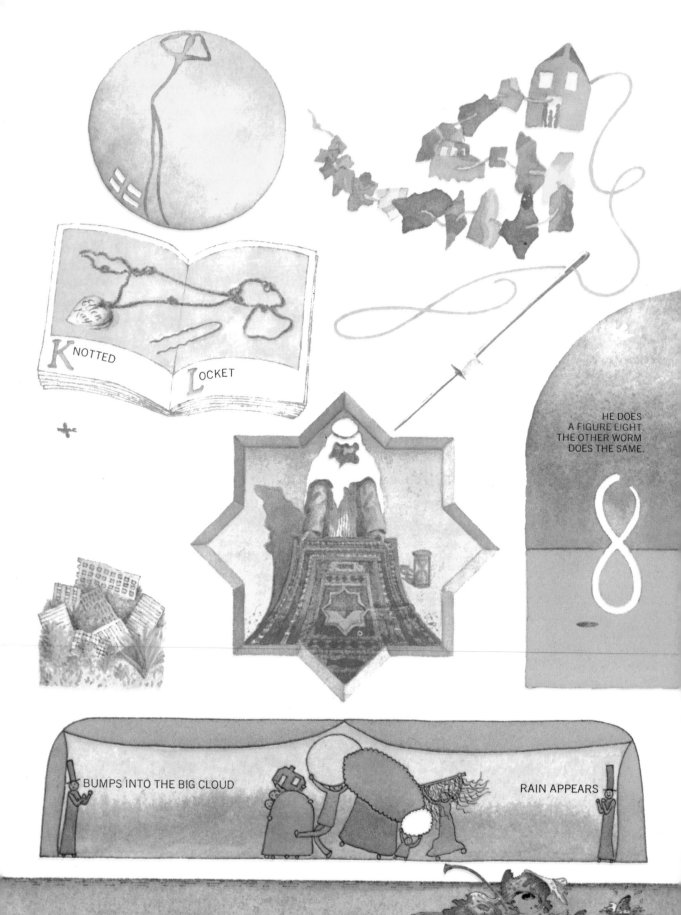

KNOTTED LOCKET

HE DOES
A FIGURE EIGHT.
THE OTHER WORM
DOES THE SAME.

BUMPS INTO THE BIG CLOUD

RAIN APPEARS

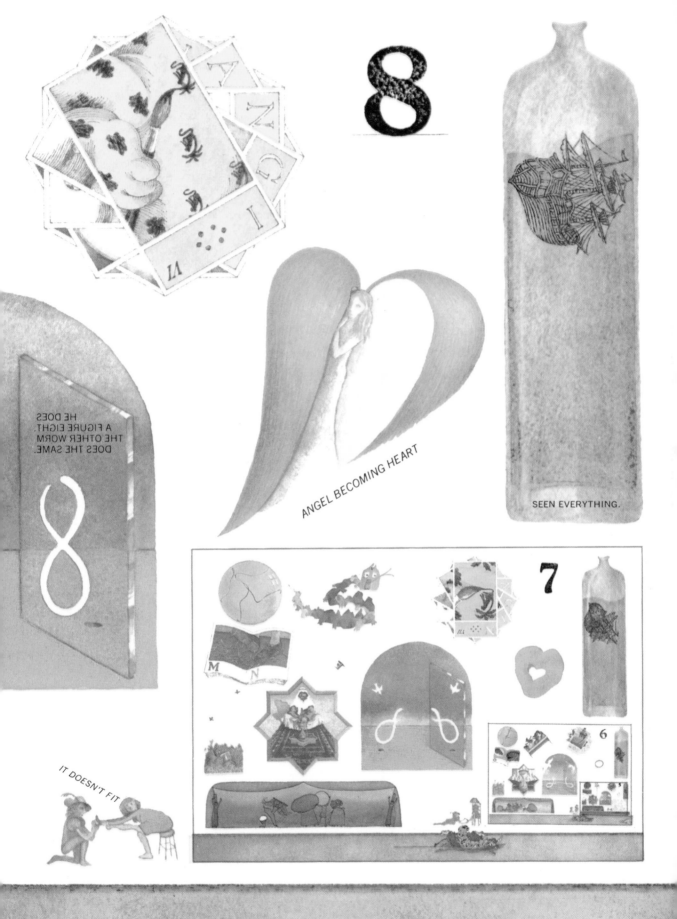

HE DOES
A FIGURE EIGHT.
THE OTHER WORM
DOES THE SAME.

ANGEL BECOMING HEART

SEEN EVERYTHING.

IT DOESN'T FIT

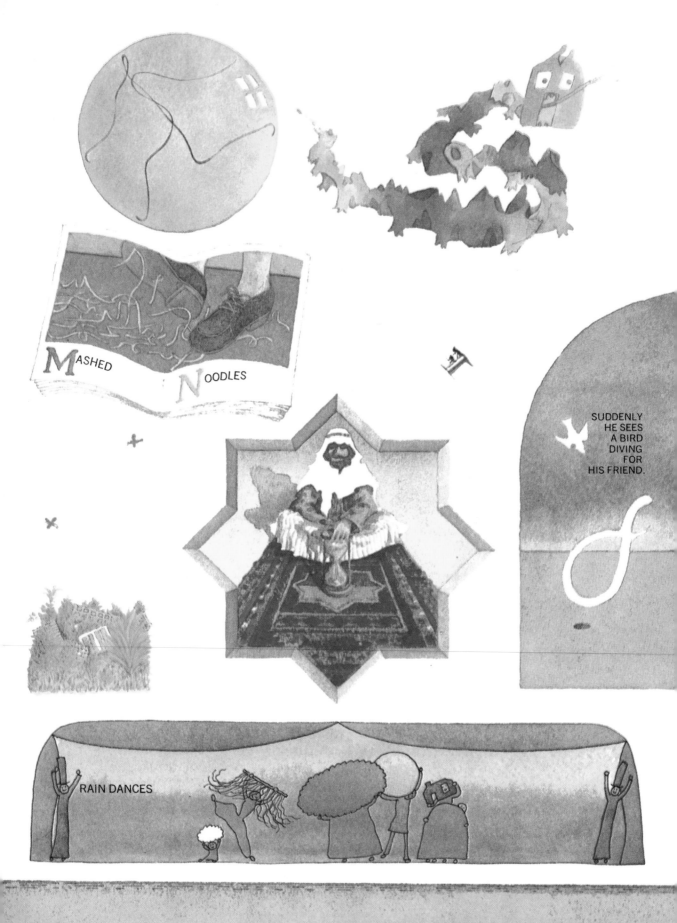

MASHED **N**OODLES

SUDDENLY
HE SEES
A BIRD
DIVING
FOR
HIS FRIEND.

RAIN DANCES

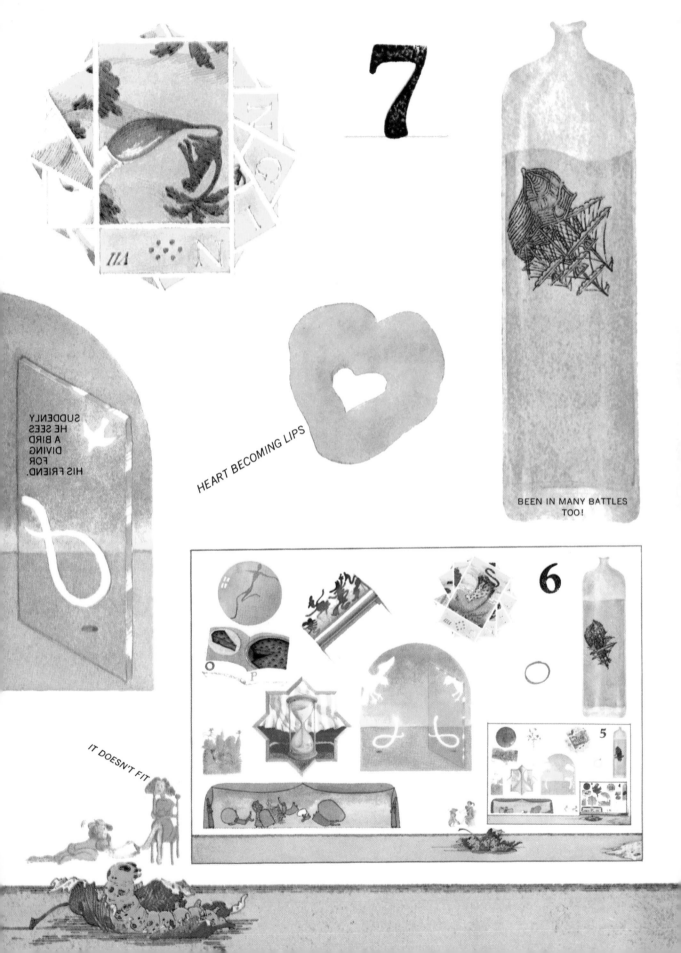

7

SUDDENLY HE SEES A BIRD DIVING FOR HIS FRIEND.

HEART BECOMING LIPS

BEEN IN MANY BATTLES TOO!

IT DOESN'T FIT

6

5

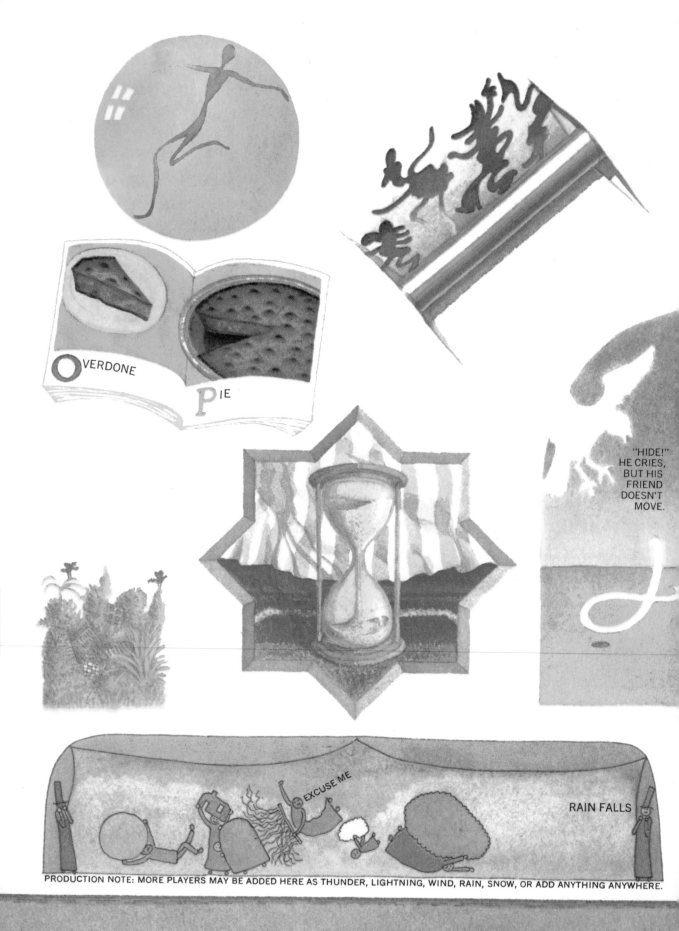

OVERDONE

PIE

"HIDE!"
HE CRIES,
BUT HIS
FRIEND
DOESN'T
MOVE.

EXCUSE ME

RAIN FALLS

PRODUCTION NOTE: MORE PLAYERS MAY BE ADDED HERE AS THUNDER, LIGHTNING, WIND, RAIN, SNOW, OR ADD ANYTHING ANYWHERE.

"HIDE!"
HE CRIES,
BUT HIS
FRIEND
DOESN'T
MOVE.

LIPS BECOMING RING

TOO MANY.

IT DOESN'T FIT

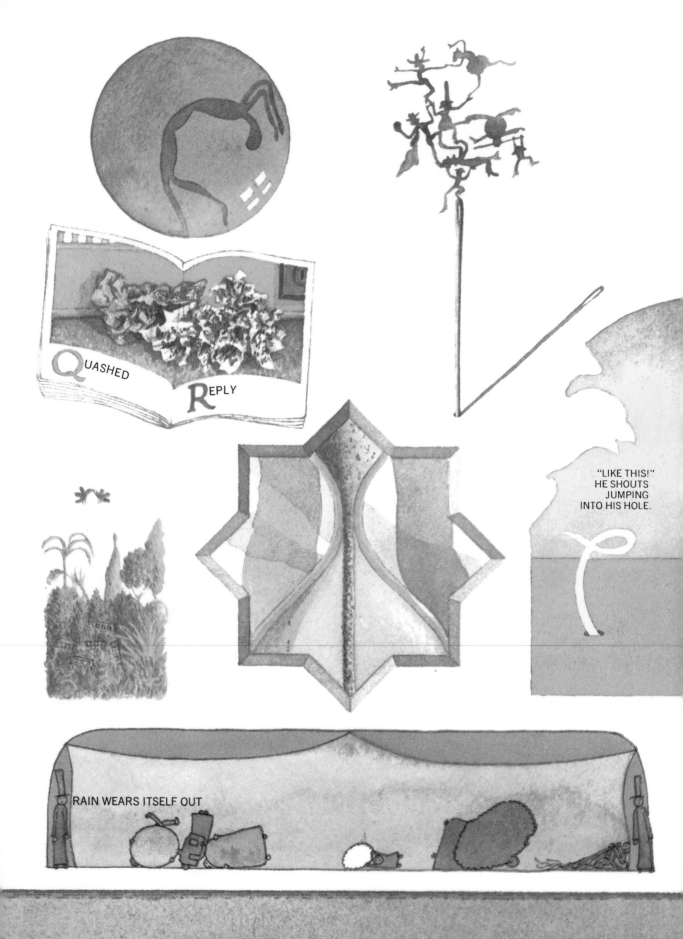

5

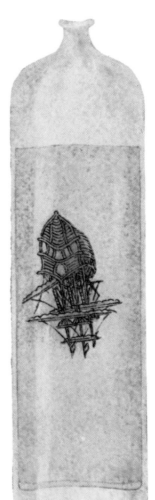

RING BECOMING LAMP

"LIKE THIS!"
HE SHOUTS
JUMPING
INTO HIS HOLE.

THAT'S WHY IT'S SINKING.

IT DOESN'T FIT

4

3

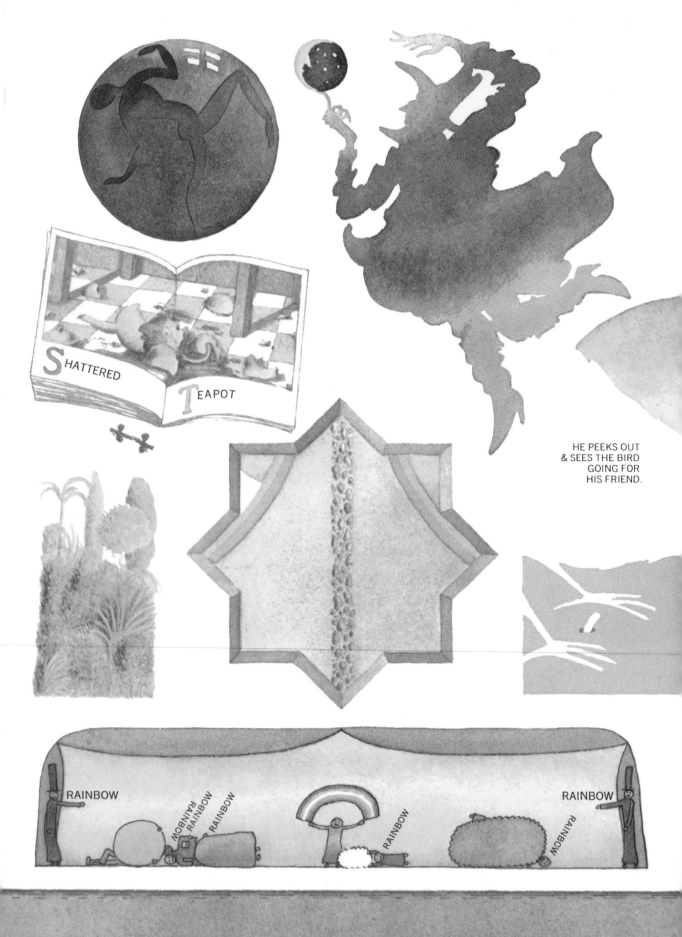

SHATTERED TEAPOT

HE PEEKS OUT & SEES THE BIRD GOING FOR HIS FRIEND.

RAINBOW RAINBOW RAINBOW RAINBOW RAINBOW RAINBOW RAINBOW

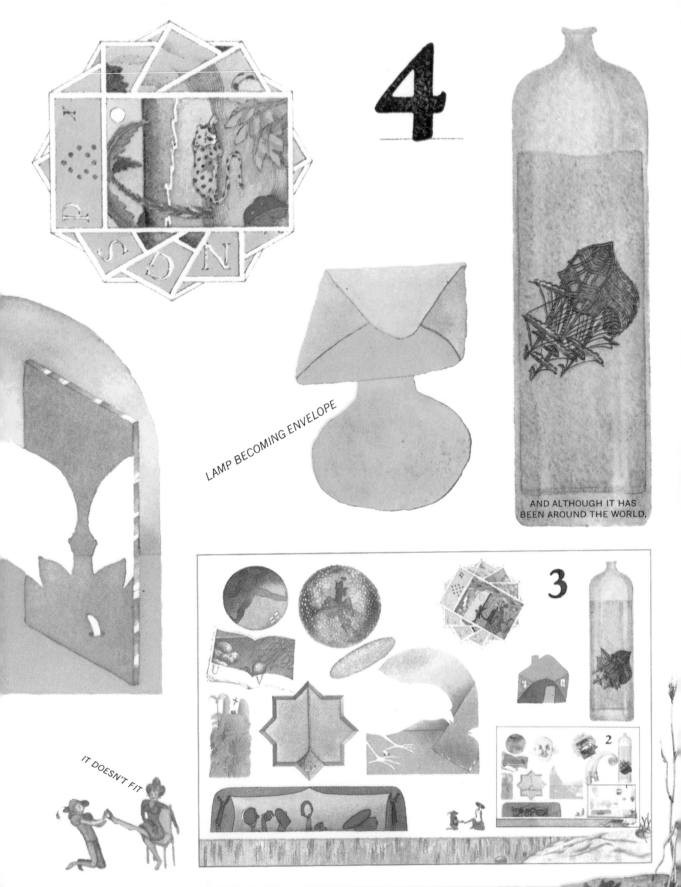

4

LAMP BECOMING ENVELOPE

AND ALTHOUGH IT HAS
BEEN AROUND THE WORLD,

3

2

IT DOESN'T FIT

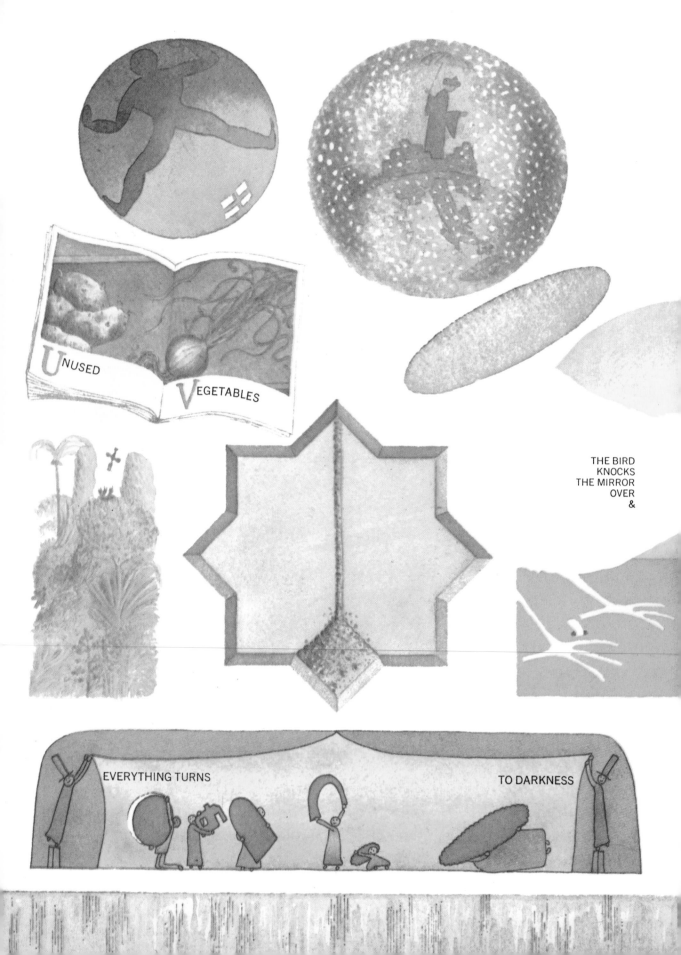

UNUSED VEGETABLES

THE BIRD
KNOCKS
THE MIRROR
OVER
&

EVERYTHING TURNS TO DARKNESS

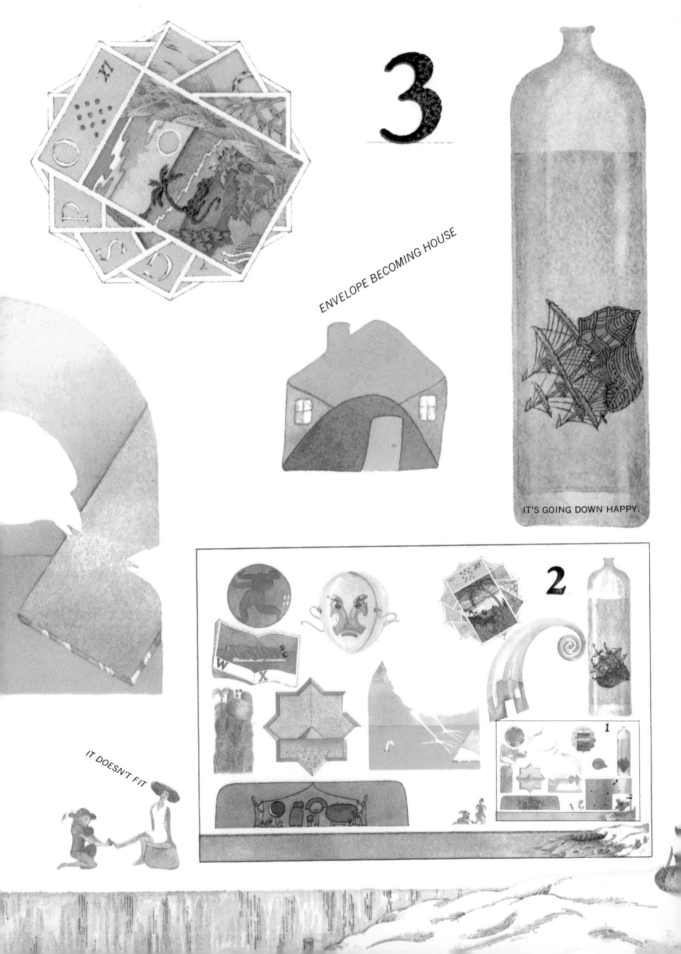

ENVELOPE BECOMING HOUSE

IT'S GOING DOWN HAPPY.

IT DOESN'T FIT

3

2

1

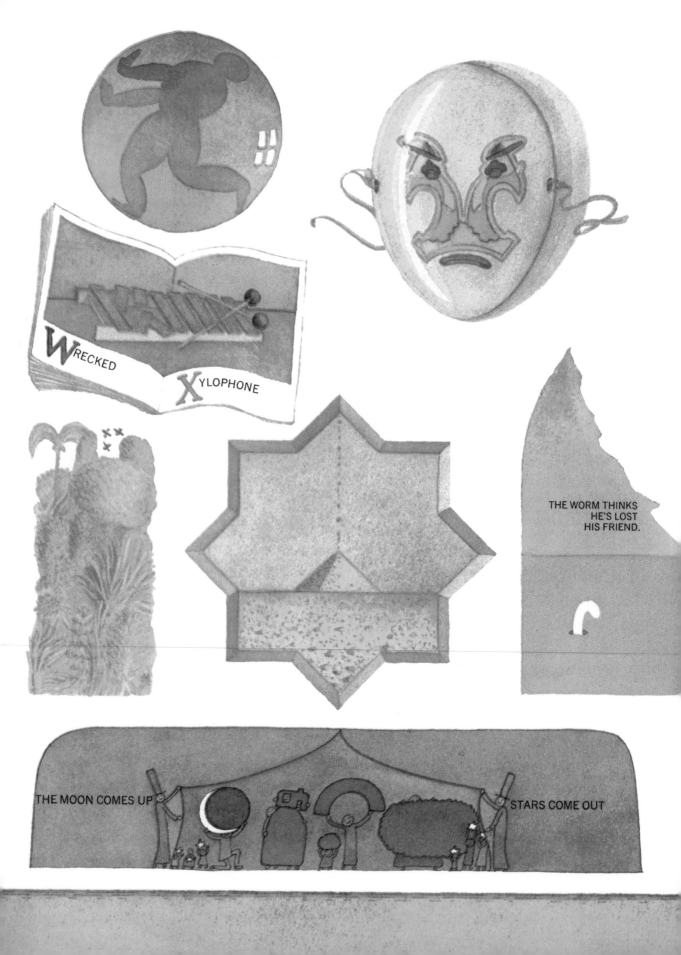

WRECKED XYLOPHONE

THE WORM THINKS HE'S LOST HIS FRIEND.

THE MOON COMES UP

STARS COME OUT

2

HOUSE BECOMING SNAIL

YOU KNOW WHY?

1

IT DOESN'T FIT

THIRTEEN
REMY CHARLIP & JERRY JOYNER

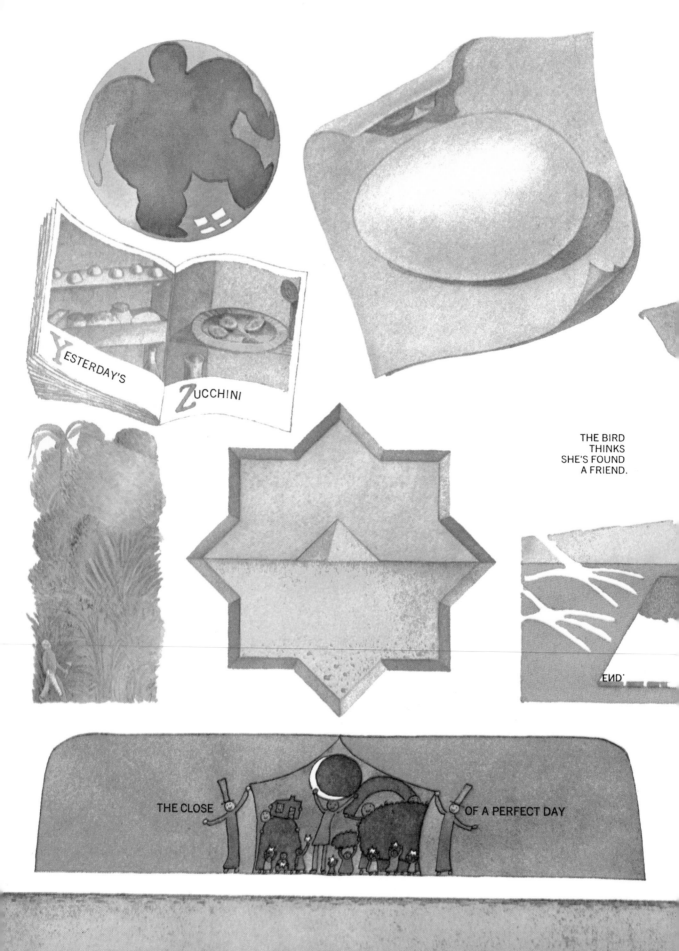

YESTERDAY'S

ZUCCHINI

THE BIRD
THINKS
SHE'S FOUND
A FRIEND.

THE CLOSE   OF A PERFECT DAY

1

S P O T S XIII

SNAIL BECOMING SWANS

IT HAS NEVER BEEN TO THE BOTTOM OF THE SEA BEFORE.

IT FITS!

REMY CHARLIP & JERRY JOYNER SHARED THE WRITING & PAINTING OF THIS UNIQUE BOOK IN UNUSUAL WAYS & IN MANY DIFFERENT PLACES. IN NEW YORK, MR. CHARLIP DESCRIBED HIS CONCEPT OF *THIRTEEN* TO MR. JOYNER & SHOWED HIM SOME OF THE ORIGINAL STORIES HE HAD ALREADY BEGUN. OF THESE *THE SINKING SHIP* AND *THE GETTING THIN & GETTING FAT AGAIN DANCE* WERE INCLUDED IN THE FINAL BOOK. THEY DECIDED TO COLLABORATE, AND IN THE YEARS & TRAVELS THAT FOLLOWED, THEY MET & CORRESPONDED & WORKED SEPARATELY & TOGETHER DISCOVERING & DEVELOPING THE INDIVIDUAL STORIES & THE OVERALL FORM OF THE BOOK. IN PARIS, NINE YEARS AFTER THEIR FIRST MEETING, THEY SAT OPPOSITE EACH OTHER TO PUT IT ALL TOGETHER, CHOOSING, SKETCHING, ADDING, CUTTING, FITTING, PAINTING & WRITING. TWELVE OF THE SEQUENCES WERE DECIDED UPON. IN GREECE, DURING THREE SUBSEQUENT MONTHS, THEY DID THE FINAL PAINTINGS. THE THIRTEENTH SEQUENCE EVOLVED BY IMPROVISATION. MR. CHARLIP & MR. JOYNER EACH PAINTED AN IMAGE ON A SEPARATE PIECE OF PAPER. THEN TRADING PAPERS, THEY PAINTED A VISUAL RESPONSE TO EACH OTHER'S IMAGES. WORKING ALTERNATELY THEY PASSED THE PAPER BACK & FORTH. THE FINAL RESULT WAS THE *PAPER MAGIC* SEQUENCE. *THIRTEEN* IS REMY CHARLIP'S TWENTY-THIRD BOOK (*HARLEQUIN*, *HANDTALK*, *FORTUNATELY* & *ARM IN ARM*) & JERRY JOYNER'S THIRD (*THE LOOKING BOOK* & *HOW FAR WILL A RUBBER BAND STRETCH?*).

PHOTOGRAPH BY RUTI PUTTI

REMY CHARLIP & JERRY JOYNER

THIRTEEN

REMY CHARLIP & JERRY JOYNER

THIRTEEN

NYRB